BOO

BOO

LITTLE DOG IN THE BIG CITY

by

J. H. Lee

Photography by

Gretchen LeMaistre

CHRONICLE BOOKS

SAN FRANCISCO

Library of Congress Cataloging-in-Publication Data available.

ISBN: 978-1-4521-0971-8

Manufactured in North America

Designed by Amy E. Achaibou

See the full range of Boo products at www.chroniclebooks.com.

10 9 8 7 6 5

Chronicle Books
680 Second Street
San Francisco, California 94107
www.chroniclebooks.com

MIX
Paper from
responsible sources
FSC® C002589

Hello, I'm Boo the dog!

This morning I am going online to plan out my day.

My favorite thing is to hang out with my best friend Buddy.

Today we're going on an adventure.

Big city, here we come!

We take the cable car to the pier.

I can see all the way across the ocean.

I may have to get myself a boat one day.

Getting my game face on.

Look what I won!

Is my head really that big?

We go for a ride on the carousel.

Buddy and I love capturing our silly moments.

Undercover pups. Do you recognize us?

Next we head to the ocean. Our favorite!

I enjoy long walks on the beach.

Sunbathing in style.

Buddy told me to get in.

I build us a sand castle.

We are best friends forever.

Now we're ready for some shopping!

This bed's too big.

This one's too small.

This one's just right—and my favorite color!

It's fun trying on new outfits.

The clothes make the pup.

I don't think this is the look I'm going for.

I found the perfect outfit for winter!

I like the fancy outfits.

And the furry ones.

But casual is just my style.

CHRONICLE BOOKS

BOO

Book Signing Today!

I like to reenergize my mind.

We stop by my favorite bookstore.

I pawtograph a few books.

I reward myself with a snack.

Yummy!

It looks like shopping was a success.

Grabbing a few more treats for the road.

Time to meet some friends at the park.

Sometimes we cuddle.   And sometimes we just need our space.

I like playing with my pup pals both old and new.

I love all my friends.

But no one compares to Buddy!

The park is a great place for a quick game of soccer.

The playground is a lot of fun.

I have even more fun when we're together.

Then we enjoy a little picnic.

After our day of adventures, we check into a doggy hotel.

Let the lounging begin!

Every dog can use some pampering.

Time for a dip in the pool.

There's nothing like relaxing poolside.

I think I'm going to enjoy this.

We freshen up for a delicious dinner.

We snuggle up.

Peekaboo!

Sleepy and ready for bed.

Good morning! Calling for room service.

We had so much fun exploring the big city.

But there's no place like home!

I can't believe I'm coming out
with my second book already! There are
a lot of humans and dogs that I'd like to thank:

- My editor **Jennifer Kong** at Chronicle Books for giving a little dog with a silly haircut a chance

- Photographer **Gretchen LeMaistre** and designer **Amy Achaibou** for working their magic on the photos and book design; photography assistants Kirk Crippens, Kevin Ng, and Victor Wong; and design assistant Lauren Smith

- The **W Hotel** in San Francisco for a posh, paw-friendly stay

  My favorite San Francisco shops: **La Marsel Dog Bakery**, **Houlin Pooch Dog Boutique & Villa**, **Chronicle Books store**, and **Café des Amis**

- My new friends: Jaida and Karl Im and their dogs **Cookie** and **Yogi**, Carolina Lau and her dog **Luca**, Amelia and Will Mack and their dog **Tess**, and Chloe and Joey Fung and their dog **Lula**

Last but not least, I'd like to thank my best friend
forever **Buddy** and my many **Facebook fans**
who brighten up my every day!

Love,
BOO